ANGEL™

NG NIGHT'S JOURNEY

Based on the TV series created by
Joss Whedon & David Greenwalt

ANGEL™

LONG NIGHT'S JOURNEY

story
Brett Matthews and Joss Whedon

pencils
Mel Rubi

inks
Chris Dreier

letters
Pat Brosseau

colors
Michelle Madsen and Dave Stewart
and Digital Chameleon

dedicated to
J.D. Peralta

publisher
MIKE RICHARDSON

editor
SCOTT ALLIE
with MIKE CARRIGLITTO

collection designer
DEBRA BAILEY

art director
MARK COX

Special thanks to
DEBBIE OLSHAN at Fox Licensing.

Published by
Titan Books
144 Southwark Street
London SE1 0UP

First edition: July 2002
ISBN: 1-84023-443-1

1 3 5 7 9 10 8 6 4 2

Printed in Italy.

This story takes place during Angel's second season. This book collects
issues one through four of the Dark Horse comic book series, Angel.

One

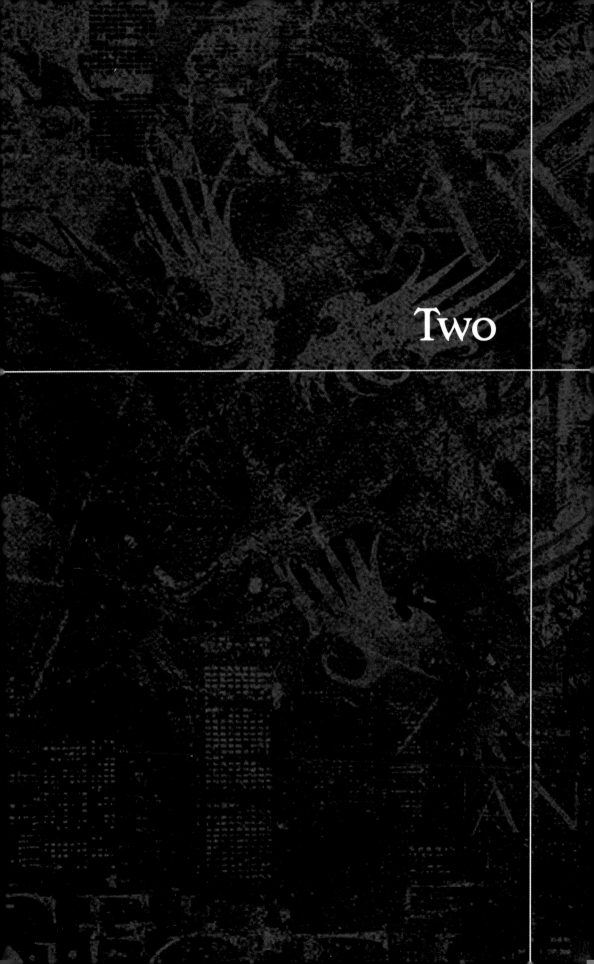

Two

-- PRETTY WELL, ACTUALLY.

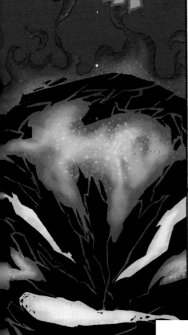

Three

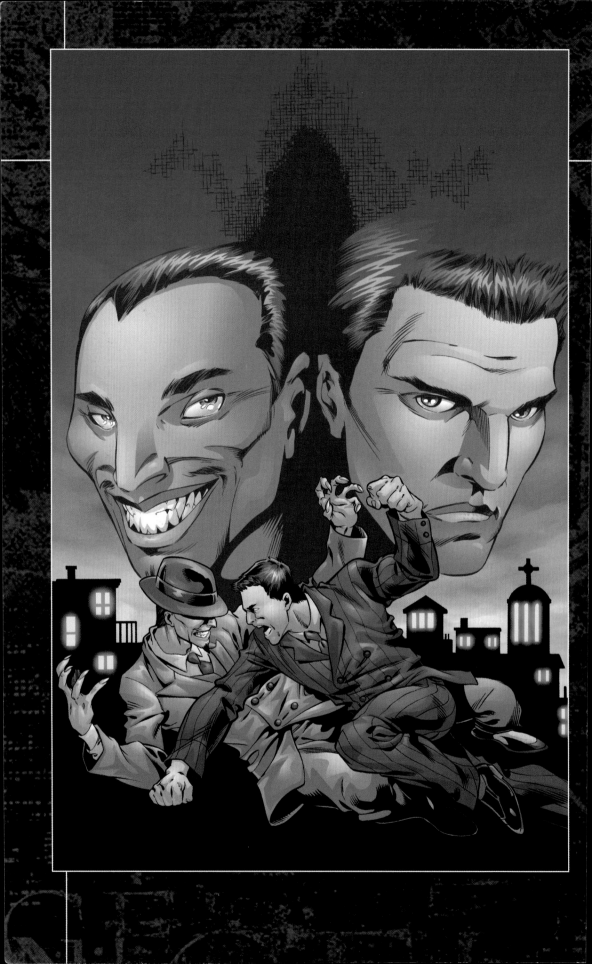

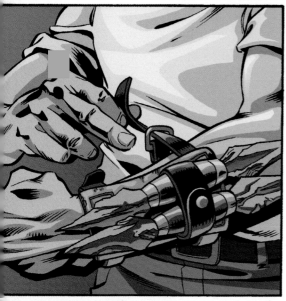

KRIK-POP-
KRRK...

NO.

IT'S
WHAT
YOU WANT,
ISN'T
IT?

PIT

"SO
LET ME
GUESS..."

Four

SKETCHBOOK
by Mel Rubi

Notes by Brett Matthews and Scott Allie

Mel Rubi had tried out for the *Buffy the Vampire Slayer* comic at a time when I didn't need a new artist. I thought he might work better for the darker world of *Angel*. This was right after Joss had told me he wanted to take over *Angel* with a new, more exciting look. So I tried to explain that vision to Mel, and this is what we got.

This is definitely the image that got Mel the job. I remember that Joss and I expected a very long and exhaustive search for an interesting artist to help define the book's new, more action-oriented direction.

Then Scott sent us this spread, and we were neither long nor exhausted. We hired him on the spot.

I love this picture. It remains my favorite Angel Mel's ever drawn.

This came with the spread of Angel in action, a quick study of the characters, which I think really does a lot with their personalities.

This is the other piece that got Mel the gig.

I really like his Angel. To me it's just the right combination of actor likeness and artistic license. And he got the hair right. Never underestimate the importance of Angel's hair.

Cordelia has probably changed the most over the course of the first arc. If you leaf back through this volume you hold, you'll notice that Cordy looks quite a bit different between the first and second issue, and from the second to the third. This was a case of telling Mel to let go a little bit, to do a great comic Cordelia instead of being hamstrung trying to pull off exact likenesses on every page. I think this is most clearly seen in issue three, where Mel and the look of the characters really hit their stride.

And I miss the long-haired Cordelia, too.

Joss and I originally thought this character was going to be blue, the reason being blue chicks are hot. We soon realized we were maybe the only two guys in the world who held that opinion. So …

Green turned out to be a much better fit for the design than blue.

Sadly.

Mel's original design for the Silthe had this real unique lower body, which didn't make for the best fighting machine. And since that was what she'd be spending a lot of her time doing, Mel streamlined her a little for the final version.

DEMON WOMAN

This was the first piece Mel ever gave me. We like our Buffy a little less trampy, but this is what led him to working on *Angel* .

The Kryll.

This design remained completely intact and the characters appear "as is" in issue one. The only difference being that they're dressed in contemporary clothes and driving a DeSoto. How I love comics.

One of Mel's real strengths is his monster designs— that and action scenes. A good combo for this arc.

At the time Mel designed these guys, very early on in the course of the project, I think both he and I expected them to have more of a role in the book. As it is, I think they make a really great looking intro. And for a bit as funny as that emergency-brake sequence, the writers deserved some special monsters to off.

Preliminary sketches for Core.

I immediately liked what Mel came up with for this guy. He had tapped into some pretty interesting variations on a sort of familiar theme.

Kind of shows you how broad this kind of stuff can get, how infinite the possibilities are. We actually chose to combine the two main designs on this page into what eventually became the final design for Core.

Core, as he appears.

I really like this sketch, and, if anything, felt like we lost some of the gangliness of the creature in the actual issues. I love the Kirbyesque feet and don't know if their thickness in relationship to the creature's legs ever really translated.

What I love about the version that made it into the book is the intense mass—any panel you see the thing in, it owns the panel.

I love the little business person about to get melted, too.

God bless Mel Rubi.

TRAILS OF MOLTEN ROCKS

— NO TOES —

— Brett Matthews
      Los Angeles

      — Scott Allie
Portland, Oregon

Stake out these Angel and Buffy the Vampire Slayer trade paperbacks